Dear Parent:

Your child's love of reading starts here!

Every child learns to read in a different way and at his or her own speed. Some go back and forth between reading levels and read favorite books again and again. Others read through each level in order. You can help your young reader improve and become more confident by encouraging his or her own interests and abilities. From books your child reads with you to the first books he or she reads alone, there are I Can Read Books for every stage of reading:

SHARED READING
Basic language, word repetition, and whimsical illustrations, ideal for sharing with your emergent reader

BEGINNING READING
Short sentences, familiar words, and simple concepts for children eager to read on their own

READING WITH HELP
Engaging stories, longer sentences, and language play for developing readers

READING ALONE
Complex plots, challenging vocabulary, and high-interest topics for the independent reader

I Can Read Books have introduced children to the joy of reading since 1957. Featuring award-winning authors and illustrators and a fabulous cast of beloved characters, I Can Read Books set the standard for beginning readers.

A lifetime of discovery begins with the magical words **"I Can Read!"**

Visit www.icanread.com for information
on enriching your child's reading experience.

I Can Read® and I Can Read Book® are trademarks of HarperCollins Publishers.
Pete the Cat: Rocking Field Day
Text copyright © 2021 by Kimberly and James Dean
Illustrations copyright © 2021 by James Dean
Pete the Cat is a registered trademark of Pete the Cat, LLC.

Library of Congress Control Number: 2020952881
ISBN 978-0-06-297408-2 (trade bdg.)—ISBN 978-0-06-297407-5 (pbk.)

Book design by Chrisila Maida
21 22 23 24 25 CWM 10 9 8 7 6 5 4 3 ❖ First Edition

Pete the Cat
ROCKING FIELD DAY

by Kimberly & James Dean

HARPER
An Imprint of HarperCollinsPublishers

Pete the Cat is excited.

Today is the town's

annual field day.

Pete can't wait!

Last year, his team came in third place.

He wants to win first place this year.

Pete puts on a groovy shirt.

He puts on a cool headband.

Pete ties his red shoes.

He is ready to go.

Pete goes to the park.

Callie, Grumpy Toad, and Gus

are waiting for him.

The four of them are a team!

Pete sees his competition.

If he wants a medal,

he will have to beat Alligator,

Squirrel, Turtle, and Marty.

Wise Old Owl

welcomes the teams.

It is time for

field day to start!

First up is the baton relay.

The teams take their places.

Ready, set, groove!

Pete runs to Callie.

Callie grabs the baton

and runs to Gus.

Alligator runs to Marty.

Marty passes his baton

to Squirrel.

Squirrel is very fast.

She gives her baton to Turtle.

Turtle crosses the finish line

ahead of Grumpy Toad.

Turtle wins!

Pete is frustrated.

He wants to win first prize,

but his team was not fast enough!

Pete will have to try harder.

The three-legged race is next.

Pete knows he can win this time.

He and Gus are a team.

Ready, set, groove!

Pete and Gus start to run.

Suddenly, they fall down.

Gus tripped on his shoelace!

16

Marty and Squirrel work together.

They don't fall down.

They cross the finish line.

FINISH
LINE

Pete starts to feel disappointed.

He keeps losing!

Next is the water balloon toss.

Pete can't give up!

He has to do better this time!

Pete throws his balloon to Callie.

She catches it and tosses it back.

Down the line, a balloon breaks.

The teams step back and throw again.

More balloons fall and break.

Soon only two teams are left.

Alligator throws his balloon.

It hits Pete and pops.

Pete is wet but happy.

He and Callie win!

Pete thinks about what games
are left to play.
If he wins everything,
he can still get a medal.

Right now, it is time for

tug-of-war!

Pete knows his team is strong.

He's sure they can win.

Marty's team pulls the rope.

Pete's team pulls the rope harder.

Alligator tumbles over the line.

Pete's team wins!

Next is the obstacle course.

Pete lines up.

He knows he can win!

Ready, set, groove!

Pete runs through tires.

He climbs up a wall.

He belly-crawls through a tunnel.

Ahead of him,

Pete sees the finish line.

He runs as fast as he can.

Pete crosses the line first!

Now, Pete is happy.

If he wins the last game,

he will get first prize!

The last game is carry the egg.

Pete holds an egg on a spoon.

He runs as fast as he can.

Pete's egg wobbles and falls.

Suddenly, he is covered in yolk!

Pete joins his friends
on the medal stand.
Pete's team and Marty's team
tied for first place!

30

Pete is happy.

He didn't get to win alone,

but sharing with friends

isn't so bad!

Pete looks at his

groovy medal.

What a rocking day!